EVERY

FEELING

B. Salone

My grateful thanks to:

To every single person that helped with this book. Too many names to list and it would crush me if I forgot to add your name. I want to think the higher power for turning my pain into pleasure. Giving me enough light to write this in my darkest times. Lastly, the ones for their invaluable comments, critiques, and encouragement.

EVERY FEELING

Every feeling is filled with erotic stories that everyone can relate to. As men and women, we have loved, lusted, fantasized, and all the above. As humans we lust a lot but that does not mean we are not looking for a connection. You see, if you can slang that slab and lay down that log constantly. The sex will always be good. I can also say that about a few women. Sometimes that person will be your husband or wife, your one-night stand, your late night booty call, a friend with benefits, your fling on the side, your ex from years ago, your fantasy, your weakness, or just straight up pleasure. Some of us have been it all or at least one of the above. Let these stories of Every Feeling take you on a trip to what you may fantasize or may make you reminisce.

EVERY FEELING

***

Best Overtime of A Lifetime

It was early fall and I was at work. It was our last quarterly meeting for the year, which was always one of our busiest times of the year. Mr. Mack, the owner of the realtor company I worked for removed his suit jacket and laid it on the back of his chair at the head of the table. The meeting was supposed to be tomorrow but Mr. Mack said he may not be able to make it in tomorrow, so it was reset for today. He had a voice that would draw you in and demand your full attention. Mr.Mack was my boss and I always kept it professional, but his chest and shoulders had my attention immediately as he leaned onto the table with his palms face down. If I known the meeting was today I would had wore panties. Imaging his full physique had my pussy going off the meter, my pussy was so wet and suddenly I was brought back to reality in an instant when my name was called. "Ashli', Ashli'!" "Yes sir." "Are you with us?" "Yes sir". "OK make sure you get those files on the bar that's on ocean view blvd and the apartments up the street from it that's going up for auction. They just got foreclosed today." Well this is great, I'm going to have to stay late because Im already working on two other foreclosure and waiting for information from the contractors to let me know if these buildings are worth the investments. After the meeting finished I was hoping and praying I didn't have a wet spot on the back of my green dress. I gathered my things slowly as everyone departed, only Mr.Mack stayed behind to attend a business call. I went to my desk to begin on the days work. I cut my lunch to 15 minutes to try to get my work done as early as possible. The day was coming to an end at five o'clock and the realtors were leaving one by one. At five forty five everyone was gone from the office.

"Ashli' just leave the paperwork on my desk and lock up my office afterward." Mr.Mack said. Once he left out I took a deep sigh and kicked my heels off. A quarter past seven, I placed the papers on his desk only to notice the picture of him and his girlfriend. Even though Mr.Mack was not married I'm sure she was happy to have him as her man. As I straighten my desk before I left, a car pulled into the parking lot. When he approached the door I realized it was Mr.Mack dressed in a Nike tech sweatsuit. "I thought you be gone by now Ashli'." "Im headed out now Mr.Mack , the papers are on your desk." "Ok thank you, I'll skim over it while I'm in my office. Oh by the way thanks for staying late to finish that, come in tomorrow about two or three hours late and get some rest. I'll still give you the hours for overtime." Thanks Mr.Mack and no problem." I grabbed my bag and left. When I got to my car I realized I left my keys on my desk. I knocked on the door and Mr.Mack opened it. "Forgot my keys." I said. As I grabbed my keys off my desk he walked back to his office, picked up a glass and downed it in one gulp. "Everything ok Mr.Mack?" I asked standing at the entrance of his office door before I left. "Yes Ashli', hand me your stapler please mine is empty." "I have an extra box of staples in my desk." I grabbed the box and refilled his stapler. He poured another glass which I believe was scotch, he removed his hoody and there was those shoulders and chest that made me weak in the knees. His physique seemed more enhanced as his fitted T shirt hugged his frame. I couldn't help but let my eyes roam down his body revealing a dick print that was tantalizing. He walked towards me and leaned back against the edge of his desk sighing. "Ashli' I um…. I lost my sister on this day three years ago, turning the picture on his desk to show me her. I never told no one here." A shallow as it seems I was glad I was wrong about the girlfriend thing and it was pleasurable to know he was comfortable sharing this with me. "Every October 3 I come in here and have a drink with her. I can still hear her drunken laugh. We had good times,"he said with a chuckle. I walked in from the doorway and I poured a double shot into a glass. "To your sister" I said holding my glass out towards Mr.Mack. "To Ne Ne and memorable times" Mr.Mack added. We toasted and down our drinks in one gulp. I had no idea scotch was so strong. My body warmed up and my heart begin to race. He turned to me and begin to speak, I looked up at his eyes and my pussy melted with the rest of me. Not hearing a word he was saying I leaned in quickly kissing him. He pulled back making me feel embarrassed and stupid. Two seconds looking at me he pulled me into him plunging his tongue in my mouth. His lips were smooth and soft, the scotch tasted a million times better as I licked and sucked the flavor of it off his lips. He picked me up using only his left arm, swiping his desk clear with his right. Sitting me down on the edge he grabbed the back of my head, gently but firmly pulling my hair to lean my head back exposing all of my neck. Between his lips and tongue I had no control over my body as he feasted on my neck causing my pussy to leak onto my pussy lips. As he nibbled on my neck I wish he was a vampire. I leaned my head further back as if he could change me and I could have this feeling for an eternity. He grabbed me by the neck laying me flat on his desk then removed his t-shirt. Every god had to have an input creating this man. He lifted my legs onto his shoulders and kissed my calves down to my thighs, He put my pussy in his mouth using his bottom lip and tongue to taste every bit of my pussy where he sensationally kissed and licked my clit. Lifting the clit up he licked all under the hood of it while rubbing on my clit with his thumb, using his other hand to finger fuck my pussy. I let out loud cries and moaned as I creamed and oozed all over him and the desk. This man literally ate my pussy so good he could have my soul and do with it whatever he wanted. He dropped his pants and I directed him to lay on his desk. I removed my dress to my feet and took off my bra, climbing on top of him. I kissed him just to taste myself and got straight to work to let him know what he got himself into. Holding the head of his dick I kissed and licked all around the top of his balls and the bottom of his dick. I took a deep breath before placing his huge dick in my mouth. My first attempt I gagged but kept his dick in my mouth and let the spit run down his dick. After taking another few deep breathes I was determined to have this whole dick in my throat. His thigh muscles tighten under me as I sucked and wrapped my tongue around the head of his dick.As I preceded to swallow his beastly manhood I grabbed his hand and placed it on the back of my head. With just a little push from him his dick was beyond in my throat and I sucked his dick like my life depended on it. His moans turned me on even more. I let him fuck my throat silly while playing with his wet balls. Nearly drowning from his dick in my throat I could clearly see he was trying to come down from the blissful state I had him in. The saliva ran down my chin as he fucked my mouth. I spit on his dick and stroked it as I rose up smiling catching my breath. I grabbed his dick and sat

down on it slowly flatfooted with my heels still on.

One hand on his chest muscles and using my other to

hold the chandelier that hung over his desk. My pussy

welcomed him inside of me, hugging it as I felt the

veins in his dick against the walls of my pussy. His

hips began to thrust upward fucking me back. I looked

down as my hair covered some of my face, my eyes

rolled back and dug my nails into his chest. Right

before I started to cum he reaches up and chokes me

which intensified my climax. Pulling out his dick I

oozed out of my pussy with a slow flow all over his

lower stomach. I collapsed on top of him, my soft

perky breast against his chest. He sat up and stood up

holding me in the air. He slid inside of me as I whimpered. He fucked me slow while I held on to his shoulders and back, secretly falling in love with how he was handling me. He kissed me passionately and all I could think of is that I will succumb to whatever he desires from me. He let me down slowly to make sure I had my legs up under me. I turned around gripping my ass cheeks making them jiggle for him before I bent over on his desk. He placed his hand around the back of my neck as he approached me from behind and penetrated my dripping pussy. I matched his tempo throwing my ass back. "Fuck this wet ass pussy" I moaned while looking back at it. His strokes became more aggressive, in fact beast like. My ass clapping against his waist, he smacked my ass with authority and reached around grabbing my throat asserting his dominance. I reached back grabbing his forearm as my pussy became succulent and I was on the edge of cumming. I moaned out "I'm cumming!" "Shitttt." I screamed as he pounded my pussy with his throbbing dick. "I'm cumming" he grunted. I turned around and gave him my throat as a thank you for taking me to this utopia. I sucked every drop I could get out of him letting it run down my chin to all over my breast. After he was fully released, he walked over to the sofa and laid down heavily breathing. Meanwhile I cleaned myself up with wet wipes that I had in my desk. I reorganized the papers he swiped off the desk. "You don't have to do that Ashli'." He said. "It's my job

Mr.Mack I said seductively. After placing the papers

on his desk, I got dressed and gave him a kiss on the

cheek. "See you tomorrow Mr.Mack and hopefully one

day I'll see you again" I said speaking to his dick in

my hand. Before leaving out I sucked his dick for a

few minutes just so he could keep me in his thoughts.

"Make tomorrow a half of day." Mr. Mack said as I

walked out. I told myself this was the best overtime of

a lifetime as I got in my car.

It Gets Wet When It Rain

Here I am home alone yet again. My husband Mike was away on business as usual. I didn't even mind that he was gone so much because of work. What bothered me was our sex life. Our sex used to be so good and we fucked all the time. Now it's like he doesn't have time or he is to tired from his flight or work. When we do have sex there is no foreplay or anything. Just wham, bam and goodnight. That would be fine if we were having a mid day quckie but Mike used to make sure I came multiple times during sex. Now it's only one if I'm lucky. My body is sexually famished and I was not going to let him tell me no tonight. I went out and got us our favorite champagne. I went and bought some new laced lingerie. I appreciated the lifestyle Mike provided us until my business got off the ground. But I am a woman with needs. I kept my body more than up to par and I do it all in the bedroom. When I head to the airport I may take the champagne just to have him nice and ready by the time we make it to the house. I'm going to suck his dick in the driveway and once we step inside he'll see what's under this trench coat. My phone started to ring. It was Mike, he must be calling to let me know he was boarding his flight. "Heyyy baby." "Hey baby." Mike said sounding irritated. "What's wrong babe?" I ask Mike. "Its a thunderstorm and they not going to take off til it eases up. Judging the lighting its going to be no time soon." He said. "Aww, I had the champagne on ice and the fire place lit." I said. "I wish I was there

baby but I"ll send you a message when they let us

board so you can know what time to pick me up from

the airport."Mike said. "Ok. I love you." "I love you

too." I decided to order pizza to eat since my husband

wasn't going to make it home. I opened the champagne

and poured a glass. I downed the whole glass in two

big gulps and refilled the glass. I was walking past the

dining room and stopped to look at myself in the

mirror. I opened my robe that matched the lingerie I

wore under it. I sat my glass down and ran my hands

over my stomach and up towards my breast feeling the

laced material. It felt even better than when I had

decided to buy it. I loved looking and feeling sexy,

sometimes I turn myself on. I grabbed my glass and headed back to the living room. I grabbed the champagne out of the bucket of ice, sat on the couch, and sipped my champagne watching the fire dance as it waved and snapped in the fire place. I slid out my robe as I finished the rest of my glass. I could feel more than a buzz and luckily my pizza arrived. I put my robe on even though it was see through and went to grab the pizza. "Hold on let me get you a tip, it's the least I can do. You're soaked and you kept my pizza dry. Im more than sure he looked at my ass as I walked away. I gave him a $20 tip and told him to have a good night. I removed my robe again and laid in front of the fireplace. I rubbed on my ass and smacked it. I started to get wet. I ran my fingers over my pussy until my

lingerie started to get wet so I decided to go get my

new toy. I cut off all the lights that was left on and cut

off the porch light last. As I was looking out the

window to cut off my porch light I could see a car in

my drive way. I crack the door open and notice it was

the pizza boy. I waved my hand to get his attention and

waved for him to come towards me. Hiding everything

behind the door except my head I asked him what is he

doing in my drive way. He replied he is having car

trouble, triple AAA is on the way and his car would be

towed away in a hour. "Ok well do you want to come

in til they come? Im not going to eat more than two or

three slices of that pizza and what ever is in the box in

the morning will be thrown in the trash. He shrugged

his shoulders and came in. "Take them wet ass shoes

off and if you are wet you can dry off in front of the

fire place." I said to him. "I'm good on the pizza but

the fireplace does look nice so I take your offer on

drying off by it." He said as he headed towards the

fireplace and took a seat in front of it. I came and stood

between him and the fire place. You only live once and

I decided to go against my better judgement. I dropped

my robe and told him come here, he came towards me

slowly but aggressively grabbing my ass and smacked

it while kissing on my neck. The way he smacked my

ass and gripped it while spreading my cheeks apart

made my pussy wetter. He went down from kissing my

neck towards my breast. I removed his shirt and my lingerie. I laid back and he started sucking my titties. Gently caressing the one he was not licking. He started kissing down my stomach to in between my legs. My back was rising and arching upward as he begin licking on my clit. My nipples became harder and my breathing became heavier. He lifted my legs and went from licking my clit down to the bottom of my pussy going back and forth. He begin to eat my pussy and gently suck on my clit. I started cumming all over his lips and apparently he could tell. He was so in sync with my body. He flipped me over and before I could look he was sliding the biggest dick I ever felt inside of me. "Oh shit" I moaned. He pulled me by the waist so I could be face down ass up then pulled my hair while

he smacked my ass. He was having to much with fun

me but it felt too good to make him stop. My pussy

juice ran down my thighs as I felt his thick dick

rubbing against my walls. "Fuck this good ass pussy" I

moaned out. He started to pound my pussy harder til I

was flat on my stomach, he reached around and started

choking me as he nibbled between my neck and

shoulder. I never been choked before and I was already

in love with it as it made me cum in a way I never

experienced. He knew how to squeeze my throat and

he knew when to loosen his grip. I moaned and let out

a small shriek as he slid his finger in my ass. It hurted

and felt good at the same time, I could tell he was

inexperienced when it came to anal because he didn't

even wet my asshole enough but luckily I did anal so I

could take a finger. I rolled over and he pulled his

massive dick out my pussy. I told him to sit on the

couch and I sat on him with my tits in his face. I

rubbed on my pussy with my hand and rubbed the

juices on my asshole. "You wanna fuck me in my ass?"

I asked him. He smiled as he shook his head up and

down. I got up and turned around and told him "eat my

ass and make it wet and nasty." He slid forward as I

bent over. He spreaded my ass cheeks open slowly as

he laid wet kisses all up and down the crack of my ass.

I had better ass eaters but he got the job done and it

had moments when it felt good. I went and grab some

lube, then spit on his dick and stroked it. I slowly sat down on it and he moaned as I slid his dick inside of me. I was focusing on getting his whole dick in as I slid down on it. It was so thick and I could feel it stretching my ass open. My hand was barely wrapping around the base of his dick when I gripped it to keep it steady as I rode it. Every time I went up and down on his dick, it felt better and my pussy got wetter leaving his lower stomach shiny and full of pussy juice. He grabbed my titties as they bounced in his face. My hands gripped the back of the couch and my pussy kept cumming back to back. This young boy had some good dick surprisingly. Keeping his dick in my ass I turned around and rode him cowgirl style. He reached around playing with my pussy. I had no clue my pussy could continuously cum and a sensation begin to build up in my ass. "Im bout to cum!" I screamed! He rubbed my clit faster. I tried to grab it to get him to stop but at this point I had lost full control. My whole body begin to pulsate. I could only shrill repeatedly until I could feel him cumming as he moaned. I was still on top of him leaning and laying on his body shaking like I was in full seizure mode for a few seconds. I was unable to move until his dick started getting soft and slid out. Even that had me shake for a few seconds because my A spot was so sensitive from the multiple orgasms I just had. On my camera I could see triple AAA pulling into my driveway. "Don't leave that condom here, take it with you and throw it away outside away from my

property." I sent Mike a message that I was too tipsy to

drive and catch a uber home. I took a quick shower and

curled up in front of the fireplace passing out right to

sleep. Who would of knew the rain from a

thunderstorm would bring me a great orgasm and have

me so wet when it rain.

***

A Laid lay over

Here I was once again, at another airport waiting. At this point, the layovers made me consider changing the way I travel. It was the middle of the night so everything was closed in the airport. I had no more business meetings so I removed my suit jacket and tie to put them inside my suitcase. I decided I would put on a sweatsuit that was more comfortable so I grabbed my luggage and headed to the restroom. On my way to the bathroom I walked past people who looked how I felt. I wondered if they were waiting on the same flight. I walked into the bathroom and went inside the corner stall which was the biggest. I changed everything I had on down to the socks. Only thing kept on were my briefs. I got dressed and went back out to wait. I pulled out my laptop and figured I do some research on something my last client was telling me about. "Its called pillow parties and they have them in New York City sometimes, so since you're living there you should check it out" my client told me. "Don't worry, it's very private if that's a concern of yours. Either you're a watcher or a participant. The participants are on one big comfortable yoga type of mat with pillows on it. The watchers sit in chairs that are around the mat in a respectable distance and watch the participants have sex. You may (as a participant) interact with who you came with and/or with other participants if mutually agreed." Remembering what my client told me as I scanned over what I seen on my screen. "Ohhhhh sounds freaky." I shut my laptop closing it quickly instantly turning around embarrassed. It was one of the people I walked by when I went to the bathroom. "It sounds kinky and I like kinky, besides it's only kinky the first time you do it." She said with a slight giggle. "You did it before?" I asked. "No but I would, are you waiting for a flight to New York too?" She asked. "Yes." I replied. "Well….Oh, I'm sorry Im Ari." She said as she extended her hand for a handshake. "Nice to meet you, Im Derek." "Well Derek if you decide to go as a watcher or a participant I would love to join you. Take my number." Ari said. As I checked my pockets for my phone, I realized my phone was in my shirt pocket still hanging in the bathroom on the back of the stall door. I ask her to watch my luggage and quickly hurried to the bathroom to retrieve it. Luckily for me it was still there. Upon exiting the bathroom Ari was right there pushing me back into the bathroom. She removed her shirt where I saw the most perfect tits I ever laid my eyes on. She grabbed the back of my neck and begin kissing me. Ari had the softest lips I ever felt. I was becoming fully erect at this point, she took off my shirt. She bit her bottom lip as she looked at my chest and abs. A smile came across her face once her eyes made it to the bulge in my pants. "Do you mind?" She asked while holding our shirts. "No I don't." I replied.

However I had no idea what she was asking but at this

point I didn't care. She folded our shirts at my feet and

got down on her knees. She pulled down my pants and

boxer briefs, grabbing my dick just past the head and

begin to suck on the head of my dick. Her mouth was

so wet and warm as soon as she put her mouth on it I

rose up on my tippy toes and placed my hands on the

walls in the stall. She slid her hand towards the base

and started sucking more of my dick. She gagged when

most of my dick was in her mouth. She pulled it out

slowly dripping her spit on it, licking the spit all over

the rest of my dick that she didn't get in her mouth

previously. She slowly sucked every inch of dick I had

to offer. My eyes rolled back and my toes curled as she reached back grabbing my ass, pulling me deeper into her throat making her gag. I grabbed the back of her head and begin assisting my dick down her throat. My dick was succulent from her mouth as it ran down her chin and dropped down on her titties. She rubbed on my nuts and either her hands were wet or my balls were wet from her saliva, but I didn't care either way because it felt so good. My heart skipped beats and I could hardly control my breathing. She took my dick out her mouth to catch her breath which gave me time to regain my composure for the moment. She put two of her fingers in her mouth as she stood up and turned around. She rubbed on her pussy and asshole while she bent over. She reached back grabbing my dick and forced it slowly in her ass. It gripped my dick so tightly and was so pleasurable my breath left my body. Her heavy breathing let me know she was enjoying it as well. "Oh fuck it's so thick." Ari moaned. I pulled her all the way back on my dick and decided I'll take control for the moment. She quivered as I stretched her ass open. I pulled my dick out watching her gaping asshole close back up. Looking back at me she guided her pussy onto my dick. As I penetrated her essence she let out a loud moan. I begin to speed up with each stroke. Her ass was soft as pillows and jiggled every time it bounced off me. Her moans turned into deep breaths that started to shake. As I looked down she begin to cream all over my dick. I could not hold back the moans her pussy forced me to let out. At this point I would have done anything she asked. I turned her around as I squatted and put her on my shoulders and begin to feast on her clit. I stood up placing her back against the wall. One of her hands on the top of my head and the other holding the top of the stall door. Inching her upward I lick and kissed her inner and outer pussy while rubbing her clit. Her legs clamped around my neck as she gripped the hair on my head tighter. Her cries were a beg for mercy as she came all over my beard and lips. Her cum tasting as sweet as watermelon. I let her down slowly right onto my dick. Her beautiful black hair smelled good like vanilla.

Once my dick fully entered her we both let out a moan pausing there for a second as we transude. She motioned her hips and I was ready as well bringing her body back and forth. Her eyes were locked on mines. I was trapped in a moment that I never wanted to end. I pulled her closer and fucked her harder. "Don't stop I'm almost there" she moaned. My dick was fully erected and harder than ever, her nails rubbed across my back. I thrusted my dick in her as hard as I could. In a few seconds, my muscles in my body tighten up and I exploded in her filling her up with my lukewarm cum. She moaned loudly not caring who would hear us and begin to squirt all over me and our clothes. Her pussy juice left a puddle on the floor. I let her down and she put her clothes on. My pants still at my ankles

and my body coming down from the sex high, she

kissed me on the cheek and said "I'll see you at the

pillow party I hope Derek." She left out and I got

dressed. My shirt was wet but it was worth it. I'll never

complain about another lay over again.

***

Life Is A Test

It seems like my life lately has been nothing but studying. I've been taking finals and I'm finally down to the last one. My professor had a family emergency and had to leave for a few days, so she pushed our finals five days back. That was the break my brain needed. I decided I would rest Monday and Tuesday, then study my review notes on Wednesday and Thursday. Friday is testing day. Ms. Pranka class was fairly easy, but rumor has it that she has one of the toughest finals on campus. I knew that I would at least pass but as the test got closer, the more nervous I got. I was not hearing of many test that was tougher than Ms.

Pranka's and I felt I just took two of the hardest finals

in my life. I needed to pass this class to graduate.

Although I was the star soccer player. Ms. Pranka

would not cut me any slack. I figured I should attend

her review for the final at 6 PM to 9 PM on Thursday

night. So as i woke up Thursday at six a.m. I started a

Zoom meeting with a company that is offering a brand

deal for me to be the face of their franchise. Afterward

I did a light workout, running for 15 minutes on the

treadmill and hitting the weights for twenty. Working

out helps me rest better and I ended up taking a nap at

eleven. I woke up refreshed and figured I grabbed a

smoothie and study outside while getting some fresh

air. That went smooth for about an hour and a half til a few girls from the volleyball team came bothering me. "How about we study for this in my dorm?" Jackie said as she stood over me with her pussy right in my face. Her crop top exposing her flat stomach. She smiled biting her finger and looking down at me as she rubbed on the back of my neck. "Jackie, you don't even take this class so if you don't mind, I need to focus." I said while removing her hand off my neck. "Leave him alone and let him study for his final." Gabby said. "Fine. I was just trying to offer some help." Jackie replied. "Good luck." Gabby said as they walked off. As I watched them walk away, my eyes were glued to their asses as they jiggled in their little volleyball shorts. Word around campus has it that Jackie is a fun fuck. I am going to certainly find out but as of right now I gotta focus. I read and retained information to my eyes became exhausted. I rubbed them with my middle finger as I rested my face in my hand. My hand covering both eyes and before I knew it, I dozed off into a peaceful rest. I woke up to a car horn startling me. I stood up and stretched looking around. I decided to walk to the cafeteria. I figured the five minute walk would get my blood flowing and give my eyes enough time to fully awake and be ready to read again. I ate two slices of pizza and some fruit as I chatted with some friends. I grabbed a bottle of water and told the guys I'll catch them later. I headed to the library and studied there. One of my fellow classmates from Ms. Pranka class happened to be there as well so we paired up and studied, which was better for me. "I'm going to Ms. Pranka final review tonight so I'm gonna go get some rest." I said. I told her thanks as I packed my things. My alarm went off and gave me 45 minutes to get there. I freshened up and walked in five minutes early. "Welcome Blake, there is a review packet on the desk." Ms. Pranka said.

There were only a few of us when Ms. Pranka began the review. More students poured in as she went on. Some students fell asleep. Some took notes and looked just as stressed as me. The rest left before the review was over. "It's 8:45 ladies and gentlemen, so you may go now the review is over. I'll be here for 20 minutes for any questions. Good luck tomorrow." Only two of us stayed to asked questions. "Ladies first" I said to my classmate. She asked her questions and left. "What can I help you with Blake?" Ms. Pranka asked as she took her hair out of a bun and let it down. "I just wanted to say thank you for this review, it's really going to help me tomorrow." I said as she removed her glasses and placed them inside a case. I was shocked at how that slight change made Ms. Pranka look different. "You're welcome and thank you." Seeing her eyes made her facial features stand out more. Her bronze golden skin was beautiful. Pilates kept her in shape and she was about 5'5 with small breast and a small nice bubble butt depending on the pants she wore. She must have seen the surprise look on my face. "Are you Ok Blake?" "Yeah. I'm good. I'm.. I'm good." "Let me ask you something Blake. Why did you take my class?" I tried to find the words as I got lost in her eyes. "You don't have to answer that, you'll have more than your fair share of questions to answer tomorrow." Sexual thoughts started to go through my mind which made my dick start to erect, and I knew it was time for me to go. "Well, I'll see you tomorrow Ms. Pranka." "Before you go Blake, can you set those boxes on the dolly by the door please?" The boxes were heavier than expected, I thought to myself as I carried the them. I remove my hoodie, exposing my six

pack. I pulled my t-shirt down as I thought Ms. Pranka

had seen me. I intentionally flexed my biceps when I

picked up the boxes and carried them. Ms. Pranka

closed her thighs together as her pussy started to tingle.

She noticed Blake's dick print as he removed his

hoody. She never been turned on by one of her

students and always remain professional. I grunted as I

lifted the last two boxes. All Ms. Pranka could think of

is Blake picking up her small frame and grunting as he

lifted her up and down on his dick. She squeezed the

edge of her desk, trying to get rid of the thought. Her

nipples became hard. "Anything else, Ms. Pranka?" I

asked. When she lifted her head, he could see her

nipples which immediately made his erection extent to full length as he waited for her response. When she looked up, she noticed his eyes kept looking down, she looked down to see what he was looking at and noticed his dick was hard. At this point, she could not take it anymore. Ms.Pranka got up and went to the door and left out. I stood there, wondering where she went, I was hoping she was not going to tell and get me in trouble about my erection. As I gathered my things Ms. Pranka came back in and locked the door. "Where do you think you going?" She asked. "I have a busy day tomorrow, I gotta go." I replied. Ms. Pranka started unbuttoning her blouse and walked up to me grabbing my erection. "I want you to pick me up and fuck me."

Ms. Pranka said in a low voice. I looked down at her,

then removed my shirt. She ran her hands down my

abs as her pussy grew water. She squatted and took my

dick into her mouth. She slowly took it down her

throat. I gripped the desk as she held my dick at the

base and sucked my dick getting wetter each time I hit

the back of her throat. She moaned and hummed as she

devoured my cock. I tried to hold the sound of my

moans, but couldn't. I slid from out of her mouth,

smiling, shaking my head. I grabbed her by her chin,

lifting her onto her feet. I picked her up and sat on her

on the desk. She reached back and unsnapped her bra.

Her long black hair hung down as I moved it to slide

her bra off. Her Indian caramel skin was soft and

smooth. Her areoles were chestnut brown and although they were B cups, it was enough as I licked and sucked on her tasty breast. Ms. Pranka eyes rolled back as she rubbed the back of my neck moaning. The fact that they were fucking in her class, excited her more, let alone one of her students. She leaned back on the desk as I slid my fingers inside of her thong. I slid them off and noticed a thin landing strip above her pussy. Her pussy lips glistening with wetness. As I started licking her pussy, she could tell I was not highly experienced. She slightly slid down grabbing my head, grinding her clit on my lips and tongue. I followed her rhythm til I believed she came as her body jerked a few times and she moaned louder. I picked her up and my strong fingers sinked into her soft ass cheeks. I slowly

lowered her onto my dick and I loved the expression

on Ms. Pranka face as I penetrated her. Her mouth

opened but no sound came out at first. As my dick dug

deeper she released a moaned with a heavy breath. She

dug her nails into my back as I begin to fuck her faster.

The sounds of how wet her pussy sounded was

bringing her to her peak. She moaned as she pushed

me out of her and squirted on the floor. It turned me on

so much that I stepped forward and let her squirt on

my dick as I rubbed it on her clit. This was the first

squirter I've had and after her water works stopped. I

went back inside her love hole. I fucked her harder

throwing my dick deep and aggressively inside of her.

The sex sounds of our body clapping took us to another level and we didn't care about getting caught for we were in a Euphoria. Ms. Pranka pussy juice ran down my balls and thighs. This was the wettest pussy I ever had. "Fuck this pussy baby." She moaned. "I'm cumming." I grunted. "Cum in this pussy, cum in this pussy!" She cried out. I exploded in her pussy filling her with my warm load. "Keep going" she begged. "What?" I said confused. "I want you to keep me fucking me while I'm full of your cum…You see how glazed that dick is. I love it and I want more." She chuckled. I did as she asked and was surprised my self that my dick was still hard. I fucked that smile right off her face as I went from slow strokes to jack hammering Ms. Pranka pussy. "Fuck! You're stretching this little Indian pussy baby. Fuck, fuck,fuck,fuck,fuck,fuck" she screamed pushing me out of her. Ms. Pranka squirted everywhere again shaking. She rubbed her pussy two more seconds and squirted some more. My dick covered in both of our sweet releases. "Your cum feels so good squirting out of me and sliding down my ass. I'll give you some more but you need to rest for your test tomorrow. Get dress and be ready for tomorrow." Ms. Pranka put her bra back on and put her panties in her bag. She put her glasses back on and wiped the desk with lysol wipes. As she put her blouse on, I would never look at Ms. Pranka the same again I thought to myself. As good as it was I was pretty sure this was a one time thing and wasn't gonna happen again. We both left out smiling. The next day when I came to take my final I approached Ms. Pranka desk before leaving the class. Ms. Pranka looked at me then at the floor using her eyes like I did to her the night before. I looked down at the floor where I noticed the floor was stiff and the color shade slightly different than the rest of the floor. We smiled knowing what it was and how it happened. "Have a good day Ms. Pranka." I said as I walked from the desk. "You better passed Blake, Im not doing any more final reviews." "No need for another, last night review was the best I ever had. I gave this final everything I got." I said smiling walking out the door.

***

■■

Controlling The Controller

"Hey handsome." "Hey beautiful." "I've missed you, where you been?" "Taking care of business and unsuspected bills. Hold on let me plug my charger up to my laptop before it die." "Ok well I was hoping I could see you in a hour?" "Yeah I'll be logged in." "Ok I can't wait, I enjoyed the last time I saw you." I ended the video call and ate salmon salad. I took a quick shower, wiped the mirror and admired how good I looked. Two years ago I was a bottle girl at a local club and could barely make rent. Now I can make in one day what my check was. I put my oil on rubbing it in. I pulled out my white laced pants along with my white laced bra. I had fell in love with my profession as an online video girl. You see this was before there was such a thing as onlyfans and etcetera. Anyways, I enjoyed doing foreplay and performing self masturbation to high end white collar business men. These men worked on Wall Street and similar places around the world. They aggressively barked orders at the people who worked for them. Although they tell me what they want and would like. Their tone is in an asking manner because we both know who's the real boss here and who is in control. I sat down and logged in on my website, I looked at myself as I adjusted my webcam. My screen begin to ring as Mr. Wonderful called five minutes early as always.

"Hey my love" he said as he smiled. I must admit to be in his mid-forties he looked good for his age. A woman his age would more than love to have him but for me it was all business and business only. I nicknamed him Mr. Wonderful because he always gifted me the best out of everyone. "Hello Mr. Wonderful, how are you today?" "I'm fine but I'm doing better now." "Are you out of town on business? Im just asking because it looks like you're in a hotel room or something." I asked him. "Yes I am, I had to take care of something and close a deal in D.C. So I'm here til the morning."

"Well welcome to my city sir, I hope we served you well during your visit." I told him. "All is well so far. It would be perfect if I could get the show in person." He added. "I don't like to assume so what are you exactly asking me sir?" I said raising an eyebrow. "Well if you private as I assume you are only a few know your place of residence. Im not asking to come to your home but if you would come to my room at The Ritz?" He asked. "I'm flattered but as I told you all the times you offered to fly me out I don't do meet ups." I replied. "Ok" he said with that beautiful smile removing his suit jacket. Just then an idea came into my head. "For an extra 10k we could work something out" I said. "Something like what?" "That's a secret" I said while licking my lips and squeezing my breast. A alert came thru letting me know a 10k payment was just made. I looked back at him with my tongue out smiling. I sent him an address. "Meet me here at ten tonight." That gave me time to get everything together. "Ok gorgeous I'll see you then." As ten o'clock approached, Mr. Wonderful called me, I looked out the window of my friend unit, who apartment was in the hood but not necessarily the projects. I gave her $200 to use her place for two hours. "Im here. I think". He said to me on the phone. "Yes I see you, get out the car and walk down the block." "I'm going to just drive down and tell me when to stop." "No leave your car parked there and walk down here." I demanded. Im sure all eyes were on him as he got out the car and walked past people who knew he was out of place. It amused me to watch him look side to side knowing he was paranoid. "Ok stop right there and come in the door that's on the right." "You want me to just walk in?" He asked. "Isn't that what I said." As he entered, it was completely dark and he used the light from his phone screen to see in front of him. I stood at the top of the stairs just watching. "Come up stairs" I said startling him. As he reached the top of the stairs I could see the relief on his face. I grabbed his hand and led him to the room that was dimly lit from pink led lights that had coverings on them. I sat him down on the edge of an autumn that sat at the foot of the bed. I stepped in front of him with my back facing him. I untied my robe, letting it hang off my inner elbow. I bent over and made my ass wiggle. I dropped my robe and I turned around slowly letting him see all my curves for the first time in person. I smiled as I looked seeing my body glistening off one of the mirrors. "Damn you look good" he said with lust in his eyes. I ran my fingers inside the band of my laced pants as if I was about to remove them. He reached to help but as his hands grabbed the sides of my bottoms, I slapped them and waved my pointer finger side to side while telling him no touching. I bent over on the bed while making my ass jiggle in his face. I turned around and I straddled him feeling the bulge of his dick through his pants. I reached down and adjusted it so it was right on

my pussy. I took his hands and placed them on my ass.

I grinded on him and started to become hot and wet. I

removed my bra and placed my titty in his mouth. He

squeezed my ass harder pulling me closer into him, his

lips were soft as he kissed my shoulder, and his tongue

was wet and warm. His erection was growing by the

second and pushed my panties into my wet pussy. My

nipples became harder as I put them in his mouth and

he made love to them with his tongue. I leaned my

head back looking up towards the ceiling gripping the

back of his head. The urge of wanting him inside of me

made me hop up and regain control of me and him. I

could see the thirst in his eyes. My thong was soaked, I

looked down at him. "Remove my panties" I said. He slid them down slowly, I laid on my back opening my legs. "Stand up and take your clothes off." I commanded. He removed everything watching me playing with my pussy, not missing a second. It shined from the little light that was in the room. "Stroke that dick daddy." I moaned. I placed the rose on my clit as it immediately took me over the edge. Letting my cum land all over my thighs and bed. I used my fingers to rub on my pussy and massaged the head of his dick with my pussy juice. I then rubbed my pussy more and spit onto his dick and begin to stroke his ego. I rubbed his balls and jacked his dick, enjoying it maybe more than he did. I told him to lay down. I sat on his face in the sixty nine position. I rubbed his dick and let him watch me finger fuck my pussy right over his face. I moaned for him to smack my ass and squeeze it. He smacked it and I slightly squirted on his chin. "Harder daddy!" I demanded more. He slapped it harder bringing me to the verge of cumming, I hopped off him asking him is he enjoying himself. "Very much" he replied. As the climax of me cumming faded away I put a condom on him and I squatted down on to his dick. His eyes rolled back and he bit his bottom lip as I squatted down to the base of his shaft. "If you last ten minutes I'll let you to cum in my mouth daddy, I wanna taste it. I slid up and down creaming all over his dick. It was not even forty five seconds before I could tell he was ready to cum, I lifted off and I told him

"you cum when I'm ready for you to cum. Do you

understand?" "Yes" he moaned with his dick hard as

rock. "Now when you do cum I want you to nut in my

hand." I said. Making sure he knew who was in control

I stroked his thick curvy manhood as I dropped my spit

on the head of his dick. I moaned how I loved

thickness of him in my hand." I want to feel you

cumming in it. Give me that nut." I demanded as I

gripped tighter at the head of his dick. His body started

to shake and he erupted like a volcano. I stroked his

dick with his cum inside of my hand and outer hand as

it overflowed. He moaned, then took multiple deep

breathes like he was in labor. That truly humored me

on the inside. I got up, wiped my hands with a towel, threw him his clothes and I told him it was a lovely session but his time was up and it was time to go. As he headed to the door he said "I hope we can do this again." "We'll see but of course it will be on my terms again." I replied. "No problem." "See you soon Mr. Wonderful" I said blowing him a kiss. He winked his eye and walked out the door.

***

Lights, Camera, Action!

The sun crept through the drapes, waking me up. I rolled over to look at the time. The script I fell asleep reading laid wrapped up in my blanket. I've been back and fourth to LA for three years, pursuing a career in acting. Things have been on the up and up for me, I finally got a lead role on a new show, and I got a new agent who got me a very nice apartment. I've been so busy with my career that I haven't had a relationship since I got to LA. I left my boyfriend in

St. Louis, which ended abruptly once I got to LA. He didn't believe in me like I did, but I needed that from him. I'm sure he missed this sweet pussy as much as I missed him dicking me down. The thought started to make my pussy wet. I placed my hands over my heated clam to get her to relax, but all that did is made her want to be touched more. I haven't had dick since I got to LA. I grabbed my rose toy out the drawer and played with my pussy till I came and calmed her down. I took a shower after my pussy stopped being sensitive to the touch and got dressed. I like LA. There were many different types of people and you could find different cultures all through LA. I had to be on the set at 11 to meet with the casting crew. My dad lived in Oakland, but we didn't talk much with the

exception of birthdays and holidays. He used to be a

person that found talent and helped them get in the

industry, but women and a gambling addiction took

him back to the streets of Oakland that he fought so

hard to get out of. He was Armenian and my mother

was half black and Puerto Rican. They both are short

so I believe this five foot height I reached might be as

tall as I get. I didn't have a lot in the breast

department, but my 36B cup was good enough and my

ass made up for it all. No matter what I wore I could

not hide the curves my mother passed down to me. I

put my pink and white sweatsuit on, the white T-shirt I

wore expose my flat stomach showing my belly ring. I

grabbed my phone, my bag and headed out to my Uber

ride that was outside. The weather was so nice and the

breeze felt so good against my skin. I told the Uber

driver to drop me off a block away from my

destination. I got me a mango smoothie and decided I

would walk up the street to the set. Once I made it, I

met the cast members that I was going to be working

with and we all talked while waiting for the director. I

excused myself to go to the ladies room. I was going

over my lines in my head as I left out the bathroom,

rummaging through my bag for my script. I walked

right into a gentleman that was setting up lights for one

of the scenes. "Oh my God, I'm so sorry" I said with

my hands on my chest. He fumbled with the light till

he secured it against his body. "It's Ok. I got it." "Hi, I'm Jose." he said as he extended his hand. "I'm Kleo" I said, as I shook his hand. He had perfect teeth, and as I examine his facial features during this moment, I noticed his dimples, his teeth were pretty and as perfect as mine. No sound came out of his mouth as he spoke to me, his lips looked, smooth, sexy, and soft. I wondered if he was a good kisser. "You alright?" Jose asked as he waved his hand in front of my face, bringing me back to earth. "Yes I'm fine. I was just thinking of something." I replied. "I said, what brings you to the set?" He repeated. "Oh. I'm part of the cast that is meeting and we're waiting on the director. You from L.A. Jose?" "I've been in the city for a while, but

I grew up in L.A County. What about you?" "No I've been here a little over two years but I still couldn't tell you a lot about L.A." I said laughing. "Well maybe when you're not too busy I can show you a few nice spots that I know about." Jose said. "Um, I'm sorry, but I don't know you like that." " You know my name and you know where I work." He replied. "I guess so, give me your phone." I told him. I called my phone from his and told him I'll catch him later and I'll hit him up soon. The director came in and we all introduced ourselves to each other. The director went over our characters that we will be playing on the set. The casting crew was mad cool and it was fun rehearsing and filming. He gave us our passes to get in the studio and on set. I was the last woman to leave the dressing room as always. Some of the cast crew along with Jose were in a circle talking as I walked past. "Hey Kleo, a couple of us going to grab a bite to eat and some margaritas. Do you want to come?" One of the female cast members asked. I guess I gave a face expression that said I was unsure, but thinking about it. "Look you'll have a good time and if you don't, you can leave at any time. It's not like we're holding you hostage." She said smiling. "I guess you got a point there." I said with a chuckle. We were learning things about each other, laughing and playing games. When they were leaving, they waited on their lifts and Uber rides. While I looked in my purse to see how far my

Lyft was away, I noticed my keys were missing. The only time I remembered taking them out was in the dressing room when I was rummaging through my purse. "Shit!" I said out loud to myself. " What's wrong?" The girl that invited me asked. " I left my keys at the studio." "That's no problem, we can go get them. "Said Jose. "How?" I asked. "You got your pass, right?" I'll call my homeboy, he's one of the security guards and he'll let us in." Jose said. "OK cool." The girl asked me if I was ok with going with Jose alone? He's a good guy but being that I invited you out I wouldn't leave you alone with any man unless you let me know it's ok and you're good. "I'm good, plus I got my mace and taser." I replied.

"Ohhhh…. Ms.Dangerous, well here's my number,

just let me know you made it home safe. We hopped in

different Ubers and went our separate ways. When we

made it there, the security let us in." It's dark, I can't

even see." I said. Jose pulled out his phone light.

"Hold on. He cut on a few dim lights. "You need me to

go to the back with you?" Jose asked. Na, I got it. Ok

I'll be right here waiting on the couch. When I got to

the back, my keys were right where I left them. When I

walked back out, Jose was sitting there with music

playing. "That's my jam." I said as I walked up on

Jose as his phone played the music. I hit a small little

dance. "That was cute, but you can't dance for real."

Jose said. "Who can't dance? Boyyyy!" "Show me

what you got then." I smacked my teeth as I rolled my eyes. "I thought so, come on let's go." Jose said as he grabbed his phone and got up. As he walked past me and took a few steps. When he turned around, I was dancing and smiling. I imitated Tyla as I winded my hips and popped my ass. After watching me for a while, he walked up behind me and begin to whined while grinding on me. I could feel his dick pressed against me. I reached back and placed my hand behind his neck. This is the first time I been close to a man since I was with my ex in St. Louis. My inner thighs became warm and my pussy began to moisten. He wrapped his arm around my waist, pulling me closer into his erection. He buried his nose into my neck and close his eyes as he inhaled my fragrance. My other

hand squeezed and pulled on his shirt as chills went

down my spine. As the song start coming to a end I

turned around and we were face-to-face. We leaned in

and began kissing slowly. We both could taste the

margaritas on each other's tongue. I lifted Jose shirt

over his head and ran my hands over his chest and

down his waist band. I smiled as I reached inside his

black joggers and pulled out his heavy dick. I removed

my shirt and I sat on the couch with his dick pointing

right in my face. I filled my mouth with spit and put

the head of his dick in my mouth. Jose chest rose as it

filled with air when he inhaled deeply. I forced his

dick all the way down my throat so that my mouth

could get wet and make my head become sloppier

while I held his balls with one hand gently massaging

them. I deep throated his dick til my eyes watered up

and tears rolled down the side of my face. It was so

wet and sloppy, my spit dripped down on the floor.

"That's wet enough." I said. I let go of his balls and

grabbed onto his waist with both hands and fucked my

throat with his dick. Jose moaned as his legs became

weak. I let his heavy dick fall out my mouth then held

his dick while I caught the spit by licking and sucking

on each side. Smacking my lips, tongue, and face with

it. I had not sucked dick in so long that I was enjoying

it more than him. My pussy was soaking wet and when

I stood up and climbed on top of him, I started

grinding my succulent pussy on the head of his dick.

Not putting him in me yet I kissed and sucked his lips

and tongue. Then I rose up and slid his dick inside of

me slow slowly, sliding down on it, looking him in his

eyes, biting my lip. I went up and down a good few

times tightening my walls even more before I start

shaking and nutting on his dick. Jose eyes rolled to the

back of his head as he guided me up and down on his

shaft. He held me as he stood up and slowly bounced

me on his dick making my toes curl. I moaned louder

as we both approached our climax. Jose pulled out and

laid me on the couch. He licked and sucked on my

pussy as I came all over his lips. He moaned as he

enjoyed swallowing me, then sliding his dick back into

me. We both watched his dick slide in and out of my pussy. Jose held my thighs and plunged his dick deeply in and out of me. "Fuck me baby, fuck me harder." I begged. José began to drill my pussy rapidly with no remorse, I dug my nails into his arms and moan how good his dick felt. "You hitting my spot, yes. Yes!" My eyes rolled to the back of my head. "Ahh shitttt!" I screamed as I climaxed again. Jose pulled out and came right on my pussy. I rubbed his cum up, down, and around on my pussy lips. Using that same hand, I grabbed his dick and stroked it. Jose took it as long as he could, but the nut was too good, and his dick was sensitive from it. He pulled away from mc smiling.

"Let me see if it's something back there for us to clean

up with." Jose said as he watched how wet my fingers were. "You gonna get me started again." Jose said as he walked to the back. As I laid there on the couch, I looked at the camera and chuckled as I thought to myself. That would have been a hell of a porno.

Sometimes Your Past Can Help You Move Forward

I always showed up to my interviews forty-five minutes early. I always tried to give my best impression. I've been waiting to get the opportunity to land this job, especially with this company. I always worked hard at my current position because you can't just apply for this position. You have to be promoted and interviewed for, something similar to making

partner at a sports agency or a law firm. I pressed the

button on the elevator to take me to the top floor. The

elevator came to a halt two floors early to where I was

headed. I was busy looking through my appointments

for today until the person stepping in said my name.

"Blake?" I looked up and to my surprise it was my ex

from college. "Brittany? What are you doing here?? "I

work here Blake, what are you doing here?" "I have an

interview today." "What time?" "Ten." Still early as

usual I see." Brittany and I were a couple at a HBCU.

We were one of the most known couples at the

university. We probably would have still been a couple,

but my career took me to Chicago and her to

California. Long distance was not for either of us so you know how that goes. So, it's crazy we both ended up here in New York. I was glad I wore one of my best suits on the day I bumped into her. She wore a black and white striped dress that hugged her body and made it look to perfection. I always loved how she carried herself. "So what's your job here?" I asked. "Well if you make it past the interview then you'll get to see. Would you like some tips and pointers before your interview?" She asked. "Please." I replied as the elevator opened on the top floor. "Good, let's step in my office." She said having her assistant get two coffees. I took everything in me not to look down at that ass as I followed behind her. Her long black hair swayed from side to side as she walked. I always knew she would be successful and there nothing sexier than a black woman in a position of power and handling business. She walked around her desk and sat down. "Are you wearing Valentino Blake?" Brittany asked. "How'd you know?" "You know I always got you Valentino for men and it was the first thing I smelled in the elevator." "Well it grew on me and I like it as well." " Here is your coffee Ms.Jones" her assistant said as she knocked on the door. "Put it on the desk, thank you." "So what advice you got for me?" I asked. "When you're asked a question be real because everyone will give the answer the company wants to hear, so give them the answer they want while giving your opinion on how to handle a critical situation on

the job. Second…." Her office phone began to ring.

"Excuse me for a second Blake. "Hello.Yes….ok I'll

be right there." "Sorry Blake but I must take care of

something. Good luck on your interview." We both left

her office and she hurried down the hall. I went and sat

in the leather chair in an office by the receptionist

desk. The other four candidates arrived as the

receptionist came and told us we'll be interviewed

shortly. I was called last and from the look from the

previous candidates did make me slight nervous. I

entered to find a chair sitting in front of two men and a

woman sitting at a table. The woman was Brittany, but

she did not even flash a smirk which indicated this was

strictly business. Her legs had a glow and looked smooth as butter. I answered all questions to the best of my ability. Trying to stay focus but all I could think about was having those legs wrapped around me. Her dark brown mocha skin made my mouth wet. "Ok Mr. Wells that concludes the interview and we'll be in contact with you shortly." The man in the middle said. I left out remembering hearing that last year back in Chicago when I wasn't selected. Now I'm trying my luck here in New York. We were told to return tomorrow morning if called. I gathered my things as the other candidates got on the elevator. I waited for the other elevator while scanning my phone. "You wanna grab a drink to take that edge off?" Brittany said in a low voice behind me. "You must be treating

since you asked?" I replied stepping into the elevator.

"My friend is opening a new spot, meet me there in

thirty minutes she said handing me a card. I headed

there replaying the interview questions and my

answers in my head. I sat in the parking lot for a few

minutes waiting for Brittany. She pulled up and I

approached her as she got out her car. "Are you sure

this place is open?" I asked. "Yeah, come on." I

followed her inside to a dimly lit bar where a woman

stood behind the serving station. "Hey girl!" They said

at the same time greeting each other. "So, who's your

friend?" The bartender asked. "This is Blake, I figured

I buy him a drink after the interview he had at my job."

"Wait…Is this the Blake? The bartender said smiling.

Brittany gave her a stare while grinning. "Bring us two

double shots of Tequila." I said. "Dang you aint gonna

introduce nobody" said the bartender. "Blake, Toya.

Toya, this is Blake." Brittany said sarcastically. "Nice

to meet you Toya." I said. "Same to you Blake." "Are

you nervous about opening up tomorrow night?"

Brittany asked Toya as she poured our shots. "Not

really, it's like the first day of high school or college as

a freshmen. Toya said as she looked at the ceiling

reminiscing. Everything is bout ready for us to open."

She said as she looked around the establishment

proudly. "Well here is to your bar being a success and

to Blake getting the job." Brittany phone started to

ring. "Hello, oh my god. Yes sir, will do. Bye."

"What's going on?" I asked. "One of my colleagues

tested positives for covid so they shutting down the

office for seven days and wants everyone tested by

tomorrow so they can be back when the office opens

back up. You will get a email so be on the look out for

it Blake." "Well, I know y'all better not be infecting

me" Toya said. "Girl, you know I keep my mask on

and I keep Lysol in my purse." "Can we get two long

islands" I asked Toya. Toya started to fix the drinks.

"Um I hope you know I'm only paying for the shots."

Brittany said. I laughed telling her "Just because you

make more than me at the moment doesn't mean I

can't afford to buy you some drinks." The long islands

were place in front of us and Brittany took a sip.

"Wooooooooo Weeeeeeee!" "Girl this shit strong as

hell! Taste it" Toya took a sip and grabbed her throat

coughing one time, "damn that is strong but you off

tomorrow, so you'll be alright." "Toya can we get one

more round double shots, I would like to give you a

toast to this beautiful establishment." I said.

"Handsome and respectable. I like." Toya said looking

me up and down. We all took our shots leaving our

face sour. "I'll be back in a minute I need to check on

some things." Said Toya. Brittany and I caught up

while drinking our Long Islands. "Lifestyle" by Rich

Gang came on. "Damn this was my jam back in the

day" Brittany said as she got up and started dancing. I

watched her wind her hips mouthing the words to the

song. She grabbed me by the hands pulling me off the

stool I was sitting on placing my hands on her hips.

She put her arm around my neck pulling me closer.

She smelled so good, a scent of honey and brown

sugar came from her hair. As soon as her hand swiftly

went across my neck, my dick became aroused. I

pulled her closer to ensure she felt my erection. My

hands slid down squeezing and cuffing that soft ass,

she turned around and begin to grind on my dick. My

dick went from grinding on her ass cheeks, then in

between, and on top as I bit my bottom lip. Toya came

in joining the party and to my surprise that ass was

even phatter than Brittany's. It shocked me when

Brittany slid her between us letting her get a feel of what I wanted to give Brittany. Toya reached back grabbing the waistband of my pants and slid her hand down feeling my dick through my briefs. Brittany came to my side and begin to kiss me making my erection rise to the point where it was clearly noticeable through my pants. "You like that?" Brittany asked in a low voice. I shook my head yes, giving her a look you could read from my eyes that I would beg for more. She placed her hand on Toya chin and they started kissing. Toya groped at Brittany's breast as I watched in amazement. I stood up, stepped behind Brittany and kissed on her neck as I unzipped her dress from the back. I slowly pulled the zipper down to her waist exposing a tattoo covered back that I was unaware of but made me find her more sexy. I squatted down at her feet to make sure her dress didn't touch the floor as she lifted each leg up. I sat her dress on a stool and made my way behind Toya. Her long curly hair ran down right past her shoulders onto her back. She had the Panama flag tatted on the back of her neck. Her skin was like a dark caramel tone. I unbuttoned her upper dress shirt and untied the bottom half that was tied right up under her breast. I kissed her shoulders as I slid her shirt off. My mouth begin to moisten as I became eager to know what she tasted like. I placed my hands between her legs and she was fully in heat. She let out a low moan as I cupped her pussy sliding my fingers up to unbutton her pants. Removing her pants took some effort but was worth it once I saw her ass cheeks jiggle with every little movement she made. I turned her around and pulled Brittany towards me so they both were standing in front of me. I started unbuttoning my shirt, Toya joined in kissing and rubbing on my physique. Her lips were softer than the rest of her body. Brittany unzipped my pants pulling them down to my ankles. "Lay on the bar." Toya said. I laid flat on my back and Brittany kissed, licked and sucked on the head of my dick. Toya licked and tongue kissed my balls making my body jerk uncontrollably from time to time. They both moved in sync like they knew my body or did this before. Brittany stood over me, I sat up and pulled her

thong down. She squatted and sat on my face while

undoing her bra. I reached up grabbing a handful of

her 34 c cup breast. She cuffed the back of my head

and grinded back and fourth. I missed the taste of her

honey nectar. Her pussy had an ooze that I loved, like

the glaze on a Krispy Kreme donut when the light is

on. I swallowed every drop she offered to me. Toya

begin taking my dick in her throat and I mean she ate

me up. I moaned as I ate Brittany pussy. I gripped

Brittany thighs tighter as my toes curled from Toya

sucking the soul out of me. She licked, slurped and

massaged my dick and balls with her tongue and

hands. Brittany pussy leaked all over my lips and

beard. She gyrated harder on my lips and tongue, fucking my face. Her voice shook as she moaned I'm cumming and releasing herself into my mouth. Her pussy shiny and glistening rubbed smoothly on my face. I helped Brittany down off the bar. Toya led us to the private lounge area, behind a curtain was black leather furniture. I slid one next to each other to make room for all three of us. Toya laid on her back rubbing her pussy as Brittany got on all fours and begin eating Toya pussy. I got behind Brittany and slid inside her. I gave her long slow deep strokes to not disturb the rhythm of how she ate Toya's pussy. After a few minutes, I couldn't hold back any longer and started a fucking Brittany harder. "Right there don't stop" She moaned. I pulled her hair and smacked her ass making it wave like an ocean. Brittany screamed "oh my gawd! Ahhhh" as I rammed her from behind. Toya looked smiling, I pointed at her and told her "you next!" I pulled my dick out of Brittany's wet pussy, and she instantly fell on her side and shook like a vibrating phone from the sensational orgasm she was having. I stood up and walked towards Toya. "Hold on let me get these juices off you." Toya said. I was expecting a towel but instead she sucked and licked it off. I can't lie Toya head was the best I ever had, she either had my toes curling or had me standing on my tippy toes. She stood up and bent over, grabbing my dick and sliding her pussy on it. Her ass felt so good against me as she pushed against the arm of the chair.

"Mmm yeah give me that dick." Toya whispered, placing my hand on her titty. I pulled out and dropped to my knees and ate her pussy from the back. Another 30 seconds and I was going to cum so I had to get out of that pussy before it was too late. I smacked her ass while she kissed Brittany who sat up. "Na eat my pussy like this" Toya said, turning around sitting on the edge of the arm of the chair, wrapping her legs around my neck. She leaned back on Brittany, who was caressing Toya's breast and kissing her neck. Her legs clinched my neck tighter as I feasted on her pussy like my life depended on it and I was enjoying it. I kept eating her pussy as she came all over my beard. I could hear her spray my beard as her legs gripped me tighter.

Once she released me from her grip, I stood up beard

dripping and turned her around. I bent her over and

smacked that phat bubble ass. My beard was soaked

from her squirting on it. I slid my dick in her slowly

increasing my pace with each stroke. Her nails gripped

and clawed at the couch as I pounded her pussy from

behind, I was in control now, and I smacked her ass

while telling her "give me this pussy." She screamed

while smacking the couch as if she was tapping out,

her pussy had got so wet at this point it was no use of

trying to run from it again. "You about to make me

cum." I moaned. "Let me taste it" Brittany said getting

on her knees next to me. I pulled my dick out of Toya's

warm juicy pussy. Brittany had me lay back on the lounge chair and begin sucking my dick. Toya was still leaning over the arm of the other couch till she came and joined in. Brittany was inhaling my dick with each suck giving me all of her throat. Toya kissed, lick, and sucked my balls as she held one of my legs up slightly to make room for both of them between my legs. I couldn't run from the massive mouth tongue lashing if I tried. The sensation rose to the tip of my dick. "Oh shit I'm about to cum, I'm cumming!" I yelled. At that very moment Brittany lifted my other leg, and Toya began to eat my ass. I kick my legs and covered my mouth with my hands to conceal the loud noises I couldn't control. My breathing was heavy and intense.

Brittany offered me no mercy still engulfing my whole dick til her lips touched my lower stomach. Brittany's saliva ran down to my balls and she fondled my nuts. Toya's finger rode my asshole in a circular motion as she licked it. I came inside of Brittany's mouth making the most noise from any orgasm I've ever had. I wanted to scream for mercy, the orgasm was nothing like I felt before, my body jerked every two seconds like I just been electrocuted. Toya licked my ass slowly till Brittany swallowed every seed out of me. Brittany slowed down, released my balls and just kissed on my dick. They both stood up, smiling, and looked down at me as I remove my hands from over my face. Now that was a blast from the past.

***

Back In Britain

I finally had some time to go home and visit my parents. I stared out the plane window as we got close to the airport. I thought about old friends that I haven't seen in years and hoped they were home so I could catch up with them as well. I stood at the carousel looking for my luggage. "Tracy?" A voice called out as I was reaching down to retrieve my luggage. A familiar face looked at me smiling. "James?" I replied. "Yeah" he smiled with his arms open for a hug. "How are you?" I asked as I gave him a hug. Im not sure what kind of fragrance he wore but he smelled good. "It's been like ten years since I seen you but I'm doing good, I just landed and I'm in a hurry so if you got some free time let's catch up. Take my number." He replied. I took his number and went on my way. As I waited for my rental car, I thought about how good James end up looking. I was so happy for him. I haven't seen him since middle school. His dark skin looked smooth with a glow to it. His waves went all around his head and I wanted to rub my hand on them just to feel them on my fingertips. His teeth were white and straight where in middle school his teeth were kind of fucked up. It was nice to be home and I thought about the people I could catch up within this month before I left again. I went straight to my parent's house. Majority of my family came by to see me, they asked me about all the other countries I been and if I think I would make the

olympics this year. I was the tallest in my family

excluding my dad. I was 6'3 and used to play

basketball in college and volleyball as well. My mom

was from Australia and my dad was a brown skin

black man from the U.K. After I took a shower that

night, I admired my body in the mirror as I rubbed my

lotion in. Although some men were imitated by my

height, most men loved my long golden bronze legs.

Despite playing sports, Im a girly girl and have very

pretty feet. I texted James telling him I was free

tonight if he wanted to meet up. My nipples grew hard

as I put lotion on them. My breast was a little lighter

than my legs but that was normal for me with the

winter season over and the spring season coming in.

My yellow titties and beige nipples are pretty as fuck.

Between working out and volley ball I gained a nice

bubble butt. James sent a location to a restaurant with a

message that said put on your best dress and heels. I

told him I'll be ready in a little over a hour. I slept

majority of the flight so I was well rested. I grabbed

my black laced thong and bra. I pulled out a fitted red

dress with tan heels that were red bottoms. "Come in"

I said as there was a knock on the door. "A date on the

first night home?" My mom asked smiling. "No date,

just dinner mom." "Well I just came to tell you

goodnight. You dressed up real nice for just dinner, be

safe, love you." My mom chuckled as she shut my

room door. I grabbed my small clutch and headed to my destination. I pulled in and had valet my car. James was sitting at the table waiting for me. He stood up and pulled my chair out as I walked up. "I ordered us some white wine." James said. We both ordered salmon, asparagus, and rice. After eating we walked ten minutes along the lake. I told him about what I been working towards. He mentioned my past accomplishments. "I been keeping up with you in my free time." James said. "So what you been up to?" I asked him. I'm a sports agent now. Im thinking of starting my own agency soon and Im starting a summer sports camp for kids." "Congratulations." I replied. His fitted suit showed his physique that showed he kept himself in shape. I was an inch taller but my heels made me a little bit taller. "We can catch up more at my place unless you have later plans."He said as we waited for valet. "This might be the only free night I have the whole time I'm here. I'll follow you there." I said. We pulled up to the loft and he let me park in his spot because it was closer to the entrance. He cut on the lights and his place was elegant. Way more than I thought it would be. He was the perfect gentleman the entire evening. "Make yourself at home" he said. He threw his suit jacket on the arm of a sofa and headed into the kitchen. His place was nice and smelled good. "I thought I told you to make yourself at home." James said. "I am" I replied smiling. "What woman walks into her home and keeps her heels on?" He asked smiling back at me. He poured wine into the glasses he brought from the kitchen. He handed me one glass and sat on the couch with some space between us. He looked down at my feet and patted his lap. I laughed not taking him seriously, he went to his entertainment system and opened a drawer. When he sat back down I noticed that he sat down a small bottle of moroccan oil on the table. "What's that for?" I asked. "Well I figured I had you on your feet more than expected, so the least I could do is massage them for you. We just friends catching up, it don't gotta be weird. Do you have an agent?" James asked as I placed my feet in his lap.

"Yeah but it's just a year trial run. She ain't done much though so if nothing changes then I may need a new one. That feels good." I told him as I closed my eyes. As he made his way up my ankle, I wanted him to rub the rest of my body. I enjoyed the way his hands caressed me. My pussy started to heat up and moisten. I could feel his dick bulge growing as one of my feet was on his lap while he massaged the other foot. I started rubbing his dick with my foot. My pussy pulsated as I stared at his dick print. He stood up and unbuttoned his pants, dropping them to the floor. This was the thickest dick I ever seen. I have had longer but never this thick. My pussy was eager to feel his massive girth inside of me. He knelt and slid his hands up the side of my dress. As he removed my panties, he looked at the inside of them and smiled. "I like this" he said referring to the clear slimy ooze that came from my ovulating pussy. I heighten my dress til it was up to my belly button and laid back on his couch. He laid on the other end placing my feet between his legs. He kissed my feet and licked my toes. I never felt this kind of sensation shoot through my body from how he caressed my feet. He grabbed the oil and squirted more on my feet. As he grabbed my feet he shockingly placed his dick between them. He moved my feet up and down on his dick and it became thicker as he leaned back and closed his eyes. I adjusted my self and started giving him what he wanted. This is something I never done before but I liked him and his beautiful

dick. It turned me on feeling him between my feet as

they slid up and down. The fat mushroom head. The

thickness of it. Those thick dick veins! I know I had to

be cheesing hard as I thought about what this dick is

going to do to me in the dimly lit cool night. I made

him place his feet on the floor and had him sit up right.

I clamped my feet tighter on his dick as I could. He

moaned my name repeatedly and I moaned with him.

He started nutting all over my feet and toes. Watching

my feet making his dick erupt with that warm cum

excited my hormones and I could no longer contain

myself, hopping right on top of him and kissing him. I

grabbed his dick and slid down the head. I didn't care

if he was still cumming or not. I wanted him inside of me. He felt even thicker inside of my pussy, it would take a few strokes before he would be all the way inside of me. I rose up and down on it, moaning as he penetrated me deeper and deeper. He lifted my dress over my head putting my breast right in his face. He latched on to my tit like a newborn as I grabbed the back of his head to keep him from releasing my breast from his mouth. His aggressiveness made me want more of him. I sped up just a little as my pussy adjusted to his dick. He smacked my ass and it instantly took me to the point of having an orgasm. I gripped the back of his head tighter as I begin to pour all over his dick. I softly cried out his name as he begin to move his hips up and down, giving me every inch of him. He sped up his pace and started thrusting his thickness inside of me. I reached down placing my hand around his throat, choking him. He gripped me tight and fucked me harder. My ass clapped as my wetness stuck to our inner thighs. It hurted so fucking good. My titties jiggled and glisten with sweat. His chest muscles begin to flex and he moaned out loud as I felt his warm cum filling me up. His body relaxed and sunk into the couch. Although I came already as well, my pussy wanted more. I told him "I want you to fuck me while my pussy is full of your cum." I turned around and slowly rode him cowgirl style. His dick was halfway hard so I held it at its base to keep it from bending. After a minute or so his dick begin to erect to that full girth I was craving. It felt so good growing inside of me. The sound of his dick sliding in and out sounded so sloppy and I loved it. He lifted me off of him and bent me over, ramming his dick in me. With no mercy he pounded my pussy. Before I knew it my head was face down in between the cushions. Our mixed juices ran down my thighs. "It's so much dick" I cried. "Take it. Take it. … Take that big ass dick." James demanded as he deep stroked my pussy. His balls were hitting my clit. My pussy started to quiver, I reached for anything to grab as my pussy started to leak. I held on to the couch pillow screaming into it as my pussy juice ran down like a waterfall. My eyes rolled back while he pulled out and ate my pussy as I squirted on his face. He stood up and rubbed his fat thick head up and down on my pussy. He penetrated my pussy and in a few strokes my pussy was pushing his massive dick out making me squirt again. My eyes rolled back again and my eye lids flickered as this man was removing my soul through my pussy into his dick. His stroke changed up and I knew he was about to cum. When I felt he was at his peak, I pulled away turning around to push him on the couch. I took all of him in my mouth and moaned as he filled my mouth with his warm cum. "Fuck!" He yelled as he gripped the back of the couch digging his fingers into the leather. "You got it, you got it, you got it" James said smiling. I released him from my mouth with a smile on my face. "Where is the bathroom?" I ask. He pointed and I made my way into the bathroom and cleaned myself up. When I got back in the living room, James was laid out on the couch sleep. I smiled as I stood over him. I gathered my things and looked at his soft dick, proud of myself. I wanted to lay with him but instead I left quietly. I enjoyed the ride home smiling as I rode on north circular rode. It felt good to be back in Britain.